W9-BQI-744

Hero Over Here

About the ONCE UPON AMERICA™ *Series*

Who is affected by the events of history? Not only the famous and powerful. Individuals from every part of society contribute a *story*—and so weave together *history*. Some of the finest storytellers bring their talents to this series of historical fiction, based on careful research and designed specifically for readers ages 7–11. These are tales of young people growing up in a young, dynamic country. Each ONCE UPON AMERICA volume shapes the reader's understanding of the people who built America and of his or her own role in our unfolding history. For history is a story that we continue to write, with a chapter for each of us beginning, "Once upon America."

Hero Over Here

BY KATHLEEN V. KUDLINSKI

ILLUSTRATED BY BERT DODSON

PUFFIN BOOKS

To my grandmothers,
Lillian Veenis and Helen Bowen,
both of whom remembered the flu for me.

(What stories can your grandmothers tell?)

PUFFIN BOOKS
Published by the Penguin Group
Penguin Books USA Inc., 375 Hudson Street, New York, New York 10014, U.S.A.
Penguin Books Ltd, 27 Wrights Lane, London W8 5TZ, England
Penguin Books Australia Ltd, Ringwood, Victoria, Australia
Penguin Books Canada Ltd, 10 Alcorn Avenue, Toronto, Ontario, Canada M4V 3B2
Penguin Books (N.Z.) Ltd, 182–190 Wairau Road, Auckland 10, New Zealand

Penguin Books Ltd, Registered Offices: Harmondsworth, Middlesex, England

First published in the United States of America by Viking Penguin,
a division of Penguin Books USA Inc., 1990
Published in Puffin Books, 1992
1 3 5 7 9 10 8 6 4 2

LIBRARY OF CONGRESS CATALOGING-IN-PUBLICATION DATA
Kudlinski, Kathleen V.
Hero over here / by Kathleen V. Kudlinski; illustrated by Bert Dodson.
p. cm.—(A Once upon America book)
Summary: A young boy must look after his sick mother and sister
while his father and brother fight in World War I.
ISBN 0-14-034286-9
[1. Influenza—History—Fiction. 2. World War, 1914–1918—United
States—Fiction. 3. Heroes—Fiction.] I. Dodson, Bert, ill. II. Title. III. Series.
[PZ7.K9486He 1992] [Fic]—dc20 92-7715

Printed in the United States of America
Set in Goudy Old Style

Contents

Just Like a Dog

Theodore ducked as his brother patted his head. Just like a dog, he thought. "Don't forget, Teddy Bear," Everett was saying, "you've got to take care of Momma and Irene while I'm playing hero in the army." The shrill train whistle called all passengers. Everett tried to pat Theodore's head again, then ran to get in line.

Everett didn't look much like a hero, Theodore thought. Heroes didn't go to war carrying old suitcases or rusty tin lunch boxes. Heroes' bow ties were never crooked, either. While Everett waited for the train, he turned to the line of passengers behind him and began singing "Over There." Everyone knew the proud words by now, and even Theodore found himself joining in the chorus.

Everett might not look like a hero, Theodore thought, but he would probably come home with a chest full of medals from the war over there in Europe. He was like that.

Germany would probably be beaten long before Theodore was old enough to do anything to help. People were already wondering which would end first, 1918 or the war. Theodore would never get a chance to win a medal. It was always that way.

He pushed his brown hair flat and searched the train windows for a last look at his brother. Steam hissed out from under the engine, a black cloud boiled from its smokestack, and the train began to roll away from the station.

Everett leaned out an open window and waved. "Good luck, Teddy," he yelled. "You're the man of the house now."

Theodore stared down the tracks after the train. He remembered the day, two years ago, when he had watched his father go off to war. Before climbing onto the train, Papa had kissed Irene and patted Theodore on the head. Like a dog. Then he had shaken Everett's hand. When Papa had told Everett to be the man of the house, he had really meant it.

It was only two blocks back to the apartment, but Theodore was in no hurry to get home. His mother would make him repeat just what Everett had said as he left. And Irene would probably start crying again because her favorite brother was off to war. "Saint Everett" was what Theodore's best friend always called him. Theodore smiled and headed toward George's home.

He walked past a row of shabby houses. Lace curtains covered each dusty window, but Theodore knew what they all looked like inside. Every house built for the factory workers was the same. Their tiny rooms had windows that faced the street in front and the railroad tracks in back. The windows were closed, even in summer, to keep some of the grit and dust out. Every room had a coal burner for heat. A ribbon of black rose above each chimney, adding more soot to a cold October sky already choked with factory and train smoke.

It wasn't so dirty everywhere, Theodore reminded himself. Out on the ranch were his cousins lived the sky was blue and there was plenty of space for everyone. Someday he'd go to Montana. Even a 10-year-old had real work there, riding the fences and feeding live-stock. Here a fourth grader was a baby. Man of the house? Ha! Theodore spit furiously into the street.

"THEE-a-dore! Just wait till Momma hears you were spitting!" Irene was standing among a cluster of Girl Scouts in front of Gordon's Drugstore. Why hadn't he remembered that his sister was going out with her friends today? "War work," they called it. He hated how important they all acted in those stupid uniforms.

He spit again, right in the middle of the sidewalk. Then he turned and stalked down the street to George's house.

Theodore could still hear their laughter as he pounded on the front door a block away. He pretended to look closely at the stained paint that had been peeling since George's father went to fight. He thought about whistling, but "Over There" was the only tune that came to his mind. Finally George opened the door an inch.

"You can't come in," he said through the crack.

"We've got work to do," Theodore said quickly, still hearing the Scouts. "Meet me around back." He ducked down the alley before George could answer.

Behind the house, Theodore hurried to the shed. He grabbed the handles of their old wooden wagon and pulled it to the railroad tracks. There was plenty of coal this morning, dropped off the freight trains as they bounced over the switches during the night. He and George should be able to fill the wagon in just a few hours.

He shivered and pulled his coat tighter, wishing it still covered his wrists. Cold weather made it harder to gather the coal pickings, but it also made people want to buy it for their stoves. After two years in the business, Theodore and George knew where they could sell the pickings. Families too poor to buy a full load at a time from the dealer were always glad to see them.

There was already a bucketful in the wagon when George appeared, muttering. "I have to quit the business," he said. Theodore stood and stared, a chunk of coal in each hand. Without George, he'd never earn enough money to get to Montana.

"Aren't we partners?" he asked. They'd been picking coal together since they first met, and fought, on the tracks. "Well?"

"Momma's sick." George looked at the ground. "She's got the flu."

"So?" Theodore tossed the coal into the wagon and bent down to pick up more. "What's that got to do with us?"

"This flu is awful, Theodore. Haven't you seen all the ambulances?" George asked. "And all the funerals?" Now that Theodore thought about it, there had been a lot of sirens lately. And funerals. In a small, strange voice, George said, "Momma's *real* bad, Teddy."

Theodore looked up sharply. George couldn't be crying! He had to stop it somehow. Since that first fight, they often punched each other in play, but George was too far away for that. Theodore felt the chunk of coal in his hand. "Look out!" he yelled, and threw it at George's head. George caught it, swore, and hurled it back at Theodore. Back and forth the coal flew, harder and harder, until Theodore missed it.

"I've really got to go back," George panted. "You

finish with the pickings." He waved a coal-blackened hand and grinned as he opened the back door of his house.

Theodore rubbed at his sore palm. Someone else could gather coal today, he decided. He wheeled the big wagon back into the shed and headed down the tracks to the station.

"How much will it cost me to get to Montana?" he asked at the ticket window.

"The price is the same today as it was last week and the week before: 8 bucks and 2 bits." Miss O'Reilley smiled at Theodore through the bars on the window. "But I do have something for you." She held a travel poster for him to see. Two cowboys on horseback stood watching a passing train. Gold and tan mountains filled the background. *See the West by Train* was written across the bright blue sky.

"Gee, thanks! I'll keep it forever!" When Theodore reached for the poster, he saw that his hands were coated with thick black coal dust. Miss O'Reilley laughed. She rolled the poster in an old newspaper before she handed it to him through the space under the bars.

Thanking her again, Theodore hurried out of the station with the precious poster under his arm. He wished he could trade Irene for Miss O'Reilley. They both were about 15 years old. Maybe if Irene had to work, she wouldn't be such a pain in the neck. Bossy sister or not, it was time to start home.

Theodore had to stop for a funeral to pass when he came to Station Street. It must have been a rich person, he thought, watching the new black motortruck carry the coffin past. Theodore ran across the street between two carriages full of sad-looking people. One woman stopped crying to glare at him, but the funeral horses just kept plodding on down the street.

Outside the drugstore, he saw Dr. Meyers. "So when are you going *over there?*" Theodore asked, grinning. He knew Dr. Meyers was far too old for the army. Whenever he was teased, Dr. Meyers would wink, ruffle up his white hair, and say, "Guess I'm not old enough yet." Today, he didn't wink.

"Theodore," he said, his voice tired, "you'd better get home. Your momma needs you."

"What's wrong?" Theodore asked.

"Your momma's got the flu, boy." While Theodore stood, stunned, an ambulance siren began wailing somewhere up Main Street.

Victory Bread

"Where's Momma?" Theodore panted as he threw open the apartment door.

"Well, it's about time!" Irene snapped from the kitchen. "I thought you were heading home when I saw you." Theodore knew she meant "when I saw you spitting." She looked at his hands and pants. "It figures that you were playing in the coal again while Momma took sick."

"Where is she?" Theodore asked again. He wasn't going to argue with his sister now. He stamped across the carpet to their parents' room.

"Don't you go in there, Teddy Bear. Momma's sleep-

9

ing." Theodore froze, his hand on the doorknob. He hated that little-boy nickname and Irene knew it. She put cheese sandwiches on the table and announced, "I'll be taking care of everything now. Wash up and have some lunch."

Theodore was almost as hungry as he was mad, but more than anything, he wanted to see his momma. He opened the bedroom door a crack and peeked in. She looked surprisingly small in the bed. He opened the door wider so he could see Papa's picture on the bed table. At an angry hiss from Irene, Theodore grinned and carefully closed the door.

The grin died when he sat down for lunch. The sandwiches looked gray and gritty. "It's Victory Bread," Irene scolded him. "The less wheat we eat, the more there is for . . ."

". . . our boys over there," Theodore joined in. Sometimes he wished he were "over there" where they had all the white bread, the medals, and the excitement. He tried to imagine the wild battle in France he had read about in the newspapers. Armies had fought in a forest while the sky above roared full of fighter planes. The heroes from that day would get lots of medals.

He knew, of course, that war wasn't all fun. Papa's letters hadn't sounded so good from "over there" and now he was in the hospital in New Jersey. "Do you think Papa's coming home soon?" Theodore asked his sister.

Irene shrugged, then said, "I suppose you want another sandwich?" Theodore looked at his empty plate. He didn't remember eating anything, but more food would feel good in his stomach. He nodded, and asked, "When did Momma get sick?"

"Don't you know anything? This flu comes on fast. Momma started feeling bad this morning." She slapped another sandwich in front of Theodore. "That's why you were the only one of us who got to say good-bye to Everett." Irene sighed and wiped the counter.

"I'm good with sick people, though," she said. "I know all about cooking for them. Before they feel well enough to eat regular meals, convalescents need special foods. See," Irene went on, pointing to one of many badges on the sleeve of her Girl Scout uniform. "Here's the Convalescent Cooking badge." Theodore choked on the grainy bread and grabbed for his milk.

"Tell me," he said, when he could, "how do you cook a convalescent?" While Irene was still sputtering, Theodore grabbed his poster and the last of his sandwich and hurried into his room.

His brother's books and trophies still covered one wall, but the bedroom felt empty with Everett gone. Theodore sat on a bed and looked at his own wall. Posters of the wild West and cowboy pictures cut from magazines made a circle around three photographs.

The first showed the ranch that belonged to Theodore's aunt and uncle. The second was of a newborn colt lying on clean hay. In the third picture, Cousin

Calvin sat on a pinto horse in front of a huge field of wheat. Theodore thought that he and Calvin looked like brothers. They were both tall for fourth grade, both had brown eyes, and both had straight brown hair.

When he covered Calvin's face with his finger, Theodore could pretend it was a picture of himself, sitting on his own horse, with his own ranch in the background. Calvin's head had been rubbed to a pale blur by Theodore's finger.

Now he unrolled the new Montana poster and reached under the mattress for his money sack. As he counted the nickels and dimes into piles across his pillow, Theodore thought about all the coal he had carried and sold for this treasure. It still wasn't enough for a ticket.

Suddenly the door burst open. "Teddy Bear, you need to go . . ." Irene began, then stopped, staring. "Heavens to Betsy! Where did you get all that money?" Theodore tried to stuff the coins back into the sack. Irene would never have come in like that when Everett was here, he thought angrily.

"I'm waiting for an answer," she said, and began tapping her toe like Momma did when she was angry.

"It's mine. I earned it," Theodore said.

"No one should have money like that when Our Boys need so much," Irene said. "The Girl Scouts are selling Liberty Bonds to help win the war. You can buy one with that money."

"Forget it." Theodore stuffed the bag into his pocket. Now he would have to keep the money with him whenever he went out. And that was where he intended to go now. "Out of my way," he said, pushing past Irene.

"I need eggs and milk and bread," Irene called after him. That was how Momma always talked to Everett, Theodore realized. He turned and held out his hand, the way his brother did. Irene dropped two quarters into his hand. "I'll want the change back."

They both turned toward the sound of a knock. "Iceman!" The familiar booming voice carried through the door. "Anybody here got the flu?"

"Yes, sir," Irene answered, reaching to open the door.

"Cripe's sake," Mr. Ames cursed. "I ain't coming in there." His low voice sounded angry. "Don't you open the door, neither." They heard a thud as the block of ice hit the doorsill. "There it is. Get it into the icebox yourselves." Before they could answer, Irene and Theodore heard his steps pounding down the stairs to the street.

For a moment, they looked at each other silently. Then Irene opened the door and together they wrestled the ice into the top half of the icebox. "You'd better get the groceries," Irene finally said, as she wiped puddles of water off the floor.

Theodore ran down the stairs to the store below their apartment. The grocery clerk was using his good hand to dust the shelves of canned meat. He was Papa's age, but the army wouldn't take him because he was missing some fingers. "The iceman said you've got the flu upstairs. That right?" Theodore nodded, and the clerk stepped backwards. The man kept backing away as Theodore came down the aisle. For fun, he rushed at the clerk. "Quit playing, Theo," the clerk scolded. "I lost three sisters to the flu last week. Just get what you need and get out."

In the kitchen again, Theodore watched as Irene heated a cup of milk in a pot and added a spoonful of sugar. She seemed to be moving very slowly as she stirred the milk. What would it be like, Theodore wondered, to have three sisters die all in one week?

None of it felt real to him. But George's momma had to be very sick to make him act the way he had. All the sirens and funerals were real. The worried look on the clerk's face and the sound of fear in the iceman's voice were real, too. So was the small shape of his own mother, sick in her bedroom. Everything had been fine this morning, he whimpered to himself.

He watched Irene cut slices of bread and put them on the toasting rack over a burner. When the milk was steaming, she poured it over the toast. Her hand shook as she held the saucer out to Theodore.

"Milk toast," she mumbled, "for convalescents." Theodore watched Irene lean against the table. "You take this in to Momma," she said. "I can't."

Now everything seemed to be moving very slowly.

Theodore took the plate from Irene, and watched as she threw up on the kitchen table. He knew that the lumps of Victory Bread spreading across the table were real. So was the sharp, acid stink that filled the room. He simply didn't want to believe any of it.

Especially not Irene's slow fall to the kitchen floor.

Masks

"You mustn't skip school!" Momma scolded weakly from her bed in the morning. "We can take care of ourselves." Theodore shuddered as he remembered the long night.

After his sister fainted, he had pulled her up into the bed with Momma. Irene woke up a few minutes later, feverish and cranky. He handed her a nightgown and left her to change while he cleaned up the kitchen. During the night, he lost count of how many times he helped them wash up after they were sick and mopped the mess off the floor when they missed the bucket. It was the worst night of his life.

He was tired of sickness, tired of the smell and the work. He was just plain tired, too. When Irene started talking about how they didn't need him because she had earned the Home Nurse badge, Theodore grabbed his schoolbooks and headed out the door.

As he slid into his desk at school, Theodore took a deep breath, filling his lungs with the clean scents of pencil sharpenings and chalk dust. He could not remember ever being so glad to be at school.

Miss Lovelace led the Pledge of Allegiance, "The Star-Spangled Banner," and the morning prayer. The day began to feel wonderfully normal to Theodore. The feeling didn't last long.

"The town has decided to close the school for now," Miss Lovelace said. Theodore started to cheer, but when he looked over at his best friend's desk, he saw that George had put his head down. Around the room, he saw that most of the desks were empty. Where was everyone?

The teacher continued, "And there will be no more school until the worst of the flu is over."

Theodore put up his hand. "When will that be?" he asked.

"No one knows," she answered softly. "It is spreading so fast and hitting so hard . . ." She shook her head. ". . . and it may take weeks for those who get sick to be strong again."

"How will we know when to come back to school?"

Theodore didn't bother to put up his hand this time.

"The office will let you know," Miss Lovelace said briskly. She seemed her old self now. "Before you leave, the Health Department has given me something for each of you to wear." She began handing out squares of white fabric with strings sewn to each corner.

"What is it?" everyone wanted to know.

"Watch." Miss Lovelace put the square over her mouth and tied the strings behind her head. She looked like a picture Theodore had seen somewhere of a doctor. "You are to wear your mask everywhere," she said. Her voice sounded cottony through the fabric. "As you can see, you can breathe and talk through it, but it is supposed to keep the flu from spreading."

"Will the masks work?" someone asked.

Miss Lovelace shrugged. "I hope so." She raised her voice. "Now all of you from flu-free homes may go." Only four of Theodore's classmates left. The rest waited nervously while Miss Lovelace called them up to her desk, one by one.

When it was Theodore's turn, Miss Lovelace wanted to know who had the flu at his home. She made two checkmarks on a list, then asked, "Who is home with your mother and sister now?"

"No one," Theodore mumbled, looking at the floor. "They told me to come ahead to school this morning." He didn't tell her that he had been glad to get away. He didn't even want to think about that.

"Is there anyone else who could help you?"

Theodore shook his head. No one.

"No other family?" All at war, he thought silently, or in Montana.

"No neighbors?" Still shaking his head, Theodore forced the memory of the grocery clerk from his mind.

"I'll see if I can get someone to stop by," Miss Lovelace said, then smiled at him. "You're a good one to take charge, Theodore." Before he could argue, the principal leaned into the classroom and asked to speak with her.

"George," Miss Lovelace called after a minute. "Please step out here."

Theodore watched his best friend's face crumple as he got up from his desk. He was sobbing by the time Miss Lovelace closed the door behind him.

"Theodore," she called, "please get your coat and George's and come up here."

Theodore's face felt like one of the masks he was supposed to be wearing, stiff and white. "Do you know what I have to tell you?" she asked him quietly by the desk.

"I think so." He took a deep breath. "George's momma is dead?" When she nodded, Theodore leaned on the desk for a minute.

She gave his arm a squeeze. "Could you walk George home?" Theodore shook his head no. Grown-ups were supposed to do this kind of thing, not kids, he thought. Not me. "We've got sick children that we can't leave in the office," Miss Lovelace was explaining.

"And George needs a friend right now."

Theodore remembered all the hours they'd gathered coal together. How many times had George teased him out of a bad mood? Who else would have named fussy old Everett "the Saint"? Who else would walk George home if he didn't?

"You'll do it?" she prodded. Theodore swallowed and nodded. "You are one special person, Theodore," she said and cleared her throat. "You can go home after you drop George off. I hope I'll see you in a few weeks."

Theodore didn't hear anything she said after the word "home." What might be happening at his own home without him? Irene might be worse, or Momma . . .

"Good-bye, Miss Lovelace," he said, and ran down the hall to George's side. "Are you ready to go home?" he asked. George nodded, wiped his eyes hard, and handed a large handkerchief back to the principal.

Theodore didn't know what to say to his friend as they left the building and walked down Main Street. I'm sorry your mother died? "Sorry" just wasn't big enough. What could George be thinking? The silence between them grew as they walked. "You want to wear your mask?" Theodore finally asked. That sounded pretty stupid, he told himself, as George shook his head. A tear dripped off his chin.

Their footsteps on the sidewalk sounded like heart-beats. Loud ones. They echoed down the quiet street.

"Miss Lovelace told me about your momma," Theodore said at last.

"I have to leave town now," George said. "Aunt Cecilia said that if Ma . . ." His voice caught on the word. ". . . if Ma died, she'd take me to live with her and her girls." More footsteps. "I knew she was going to die, Theodore."

But *my* momma isn't going to die, Theodore argued silently. At least I don't think she will. Does that mean she won't? he wondered. I don't want her to die! he thought fiercely.

He did not want to be here, either, walking with George. He wanted to be home, to see his mother's smile, to touch her soft hand. His footsteps got faster.

"I don't want to go home," said George. "I don't want to see her dead." Theodore wanted to scream Hurry, hurry, when George fell behind. Instead, he slowed his steps to match, though his heartbeats still raced ahead.

"You can have the wagon," George said when they got near his door. "My half of the business is yours, too."

"I'll send for you when I get to Montana," Theodore said. "I'll be going soon. I've almost got enough money. There's plenty of work for boys on the ranch. Especially strong ones like us." He knew he was babbling, but he couldn't stop. "We can ride together in the roundup and rope calves and break horses and camp under the stars and . . ."

"Is there flu in Montana?" George interrupted.

Theodore shrugged. "Who knows? I'll send for you from the ranch. Count on it." He punched George softly in the chest.

"I know you will. 'Bye, partner."

"George," Theodore said as his best friend turned to go in, "about your momma. I'm sorry." It wasn't enough, but it was all he could offer.

"I know," George answered, and punched him back, gently. Sorry wasn't much, Theodore realized, but it had helped some.

When George's door closed, Theodore wheeled and ran up Station Street. He pushed through a crowd of people waiting for the trolley. "What in tarnation?" a man yelled. "Stop, you hooligan!" another called after him. Theodore didn't stop until he'd pounded up the stairs and run into his apartment.

"Momma, Momma!" he called. Irene stared at him from the sofa, her mouth and eyes the shape of O's. "Momma!" Theodore cried again, and ran into the bedroom. Her face was pale and her eyes were dark shadows, but his mother was sitting up, holding her arms out to him. Theodore climbed onto the bed, and hugged her with every bit of his strength.

Mustard Plasters

When his mother had fallen asleep, Theodore felt her forehead. Even he could tell it was very hot. He soaked a washcloth in cold water. When he pressed it to her face, she sighed and opened her eyes. They looked dull and empty. "Mom?" Theodore asked, worried. "Momma?" She closed her eyes again.

He should call Dr. Meyers, he thought, but the nearest phone was at the drugstore. He shouldn't leave Irene and Momma alone that long. Maybe they were just sleeping. If anything else happened, he promised himself, he'd go for help.

Whenever they staggered out of bed to throw up during the afternoon, he helped them to the bathroom and then back to bed. Each time, he fixed a new cool cloth for their faces before he cleaned up the spattered bathroom.

Finally Theodore sat down to rest in his father's leather chair by the front door. He knew he needed food and he needed help, but most of all he needed rest. He closed his eyes and was falling asleep when a sharp knock sounded.

"Theodore," a thin voice called. "It's Mrs. Gordon. Can I come in?" What was the druggist's wife doing here? Theodore wondered. But she was Irene's Girl Scout leader, too.

"My sister is sick . . ." he began as he opened the door.

"I know." Mrs. Gordon pushed her way past him. "Miss Lovelace sent me to look in on you, Theodore. Where are they?" Before Theodore could answer, the druggist's wife had swept past him and into the bedroom. He caught up and saw Mrs. Gordon pressing her small, wrinkled hand against Irene's forehead and crooning, "Oh, you poor darling." Irene mumbled in her sleep.

"Theodore, why don't these women have mustard plasters?" Mrs. Gordon asked sharply, yanking the sheets and blankets flat and tight up under their chins. "And why isn't the vapor lamp lit? Land sakes, it stinks in here!"

"I don't know how . . ." he tried to explain.

"Yet," she snapped. "You don't know how *yet.* I'll show you. First we'll have a cup of coffee." No one had ever offered him coffee before. That was something adults drank after the kids had left the table. When Mrs. Gordon asked him to reach the coffee beans, Theodore realized that he was taller than she.

"The sugar's in the cupboard, Mrs. Gordon, behind the oatmeal," he told her. Sugar was hard to get, because most of it was sent to Our Boys Over There. It seemed right to offer the treat to Irene's Girl Scout leader now.

She smiled and put the beans into the grinder, and told him to light the stove.

"I can't," he said. Actually, he wasn't allowed to touch the stove, but that didn't seem to be the kind of thing she'd want to hear.

"Can't?" she exclaimed. "Nonsense. You can do *anything* you put your mind to. Here are the matches." When the burner caught with a whoosh of flame that nearly singed his eyebrows, Mrs. Gordon didn't seem to notice.

Within minutes, she was pouring him a cup of coffee. Theodore burned his lip with the first swallow, but he liked the strong, bitter flavor. Mrs. Gordon was watching him over her cup. "Tell me what you've done for them," she asked. Then she listened quietly, nodding.

"Nobody really knows what stops the flu, so they're

trying anything," she finally said. "Some folks are hanging sheets soaked in vinegar water over their door-ways. Others think laying big panfuls of hot fried onions on the sick folks' backs will help. I even heard that eating hot-pepper sandwiches will help!" She rolled her eyes and shook her head. "Seems the nastier a treatment is, the more folks believe it will work. I don't hold with those ideas, but I can show you what I do know."

She laid her hand on his arm. "Before we start, Theo, I do have some news for you. A call came from the army. Your brother has the flu, too. He said to tell you he won't be earning any medals for a while."

"Not Everett!" Theodore almost shouted. Then, more quietly, he asked, "They have the flu in the army?"

"The flu is everywhere, honey. People are sick all over the world. It looks like more people are going to be killed by this flu than by the war."

Theodore thought about George's mother. "Let's take care of Momma," he said, getting up from the table. Mrs. Gordon gave him a quick hug. He could see why Irene liked being in her Girl Scout troop.

"We'll have mustard plasters on both of them in three shakes of a lamb's tail." While she mixed flour, water, and mustard powder in a big bowl, Theodore spread newspapers on the table. The mustard smell filled the kitchen as they laid two large squares of cloth on the papers. Theodore held his nose. "Just pretend you are making a sandwich," Mrs. Gordon laughed, and they spread the yellow paste on the cloths and covered them with more fabric.

"This gives a body heat," she explained as they carried the plasters into the bedroom. "The heat helps to break a fever and makes the breathing easier, too." Irene mumbled in her sleep as Mrs. Gordon gently unbuttoned the top of her nightgown. Theodore quickly looked at the ceiling, then looked back. Then he looked at the floor. He had never even seen Irene's feet naked. He swallowed hard. "I can't do that," he whispered to Mrs. Gordon.

"Nonsense. You can do whatever you put your mind to." Theodore stared as she helped Irene shift over onto her stomach. When the plaster was smoothed over his sister's back, Mrs. Gordon said to him, "It's your turn now."

Theodore looked at his mother. The plaster in his hands felt hot. So did his face. He took a deep breath, told his dazed mother what he was going to do, and finally pressed the plaster along her back. While Mrs. Gordon pulled the covers up over the sleepers, Theodore turned quickly and left the room. In the kitchen he gasped with relief. At least that was over.

"You'll have to take those plasters off in about half an hour, Theodore," Mrs. Gordon said. "Longer than that will burn their skin."

Theodore slumped into a chair. "You're not going to stay?" Suddenly he felt very tired again.

"Oh, no, honey. You can handle things here." She sat across the kitchen table from him. "I visit homes with far more need than this one." She told him to change the sheets when the fevers broke and the sweating started. She said that fevers much higher than these make the mind wander. "Don't mind whatever they say then, it won't mean a thing," she told him as she measured strong-smelling camphor into a little dish. She showed him how to fit the dish over a tiny kerosene lamp, then told him to light it as soon as she left.

I'm just a kid, Theodore wanted to yell at her. But Mrs. Gordon didn't seem to think so. Don't leave me here, he wanted to scream. But Mrs. Gordon was putting on her coat. She gave him another quick hug before she swept out the door.

With the vapor lamp adding hot camphor smells to the stink of mustard and old vomit, it was hard to breathe in the apartment. Theodore knew not to open a window because drafts were dangerous. He just sat in the chair beside his mother's bed, watching the clock and trying not to breathe too deeply.

When half an hour passed, he blew out the lamp and pulled off the mustard plasters. "Theodore?" his mother asked weakly.

"Momma, are you awake?" Theodore wasn't sure.

"Who was here? Did I see Mrs. Gordon and Everett?"

"That was Mrs. Gordon, Momma, but Everett isn't here."

"I did hear his name, didn't I?" Then Theodore remembered the news.

"Everett got to the army camp okay, Momma, but now he's sick there with the flu. He called and told them at the drugstore."

She began to cry in long gasping sobs. "Mom. It's okay, Momma." He patted her arm gently. When she began coughing, he ran for a handkerchief. She coughed and gagged into the white cloth until it was soaked. All Theodore could think to do was rub her back.

When she finally could ask for water, he brought a glass and held her head up so she could drink. She closed her eyes and fell asleep, her cheek against his hand. Theodore settled back into the chair and fell asleep at last.

The apartment was dark when he woke up. Irene was still mumbling in her sleep, but his momma was breathing in long gurgling snores. Every breath ended in a choking cough. It sounded to Theodore like she was dying.

George's mother had died. Theodore couldn't let it happen to his own momma. He found his coat in the dark and pulled it on as he ran out the door. It didn't matter what time it was. He had to get help. He needed Dr. Meyers, and he needed him now.

Escape

Theodore ran down the sidewalk through the frosty darkness. His breath steamed in the air. Miss O'Reilley will know where to find Dr. Meyers, he promised himself. The railroad tracks were quiet and the station was dark when he got there. By the half-light of the moon, he could read the clock. It was three in the morning! Theodore whistled softly. He burst through the doors, calling, "Miss O'Reilley!" The station was empty, and on the ticket seller's cage a note was pinned saying, "Gone home sick." It was signed "Henry."

"Henry?" Theodore stared at the note for a moment,

then shook his head to clear the groggy confusion away. Of course Miss O'Reilley wasn't there! Nobody worked both day and night shifts. Theodore knew he had to think more clearly if he was ever going to help his momma.

Theodore ran out of the building and looked down Station Street. The hospital was seven blocks away. He shivered and started walking as fast as he could. He had never been there. Irene said that people only went to hospitals to die.

A wagon rumbled up beside him. "What're ya doing out so early, lad?" a kindly voice asked. Theodore looked up at an old man pulling hard on the reins to hold his team steady.

"I need a ride to the hospital, sir. You going that way?" The driver nodded and moved over on the bench. Theodore pulled himself up to the seat as the wagon jolted forward.

"That's where we're headin'," the driver said. "We come in from the farm." Theodore looked around to see who "we" was. In the bed of the wagon were three thick bundles of blankets wrapped in rugs. At the end of each, moonlight shimmered on pale hair. "My wife, my daughter, and her husband," the farmer said. Theodore watched the bundles all the way to the hospital. None of them moved.

He jumped out as soon as the wagon slowed, ran through the hospital door, and stood, blinking. He had never seen so many electric lights in one place.

Or, he realized as he looked around, so many sick people. There were people lying on cots against the walls, people slumped in chairs, even people lying on the floor. A woman wearing a dirty white apron and a mask hurried past him. "Wait, please!" he said quickly. She whirled to face him. "My momma's sick."

"What do you want me to do about it?" Theodore was so startled, he didn't know how to answer her. She rubbed her eyes. "I'm sorry," she said. "Everyone in town seems to have the flu. I've been working since yesterday morning and they just keep coming . . ."

"Theodore!" Dr. Meyers's voice carried down the hallway. Theodore made his way down the hall, careful not to step on anyone.

"Momma's real bad," he told Dr. Meyers. "You've got to come to the house."

The old doctor looked at him over a girl who was throwing up into a bowl and shook his head. "Look around, Theodore. I can't leave. I can't even tell you to bring your mother here. There just isn't room."

"But . . ." Theodore began. Down the hall, someone started screaming about spiders.

"Don't listen, Theodore," Dr. Meyers said. "It's just her fever talking. Is your mother doing that yet?" Theodore shook his head. Somewhere a man began moaning and a little boy started throwing up.

Theodore tried not to hear anything else in the hospital. "No. But she can't breathe very well."

"Listen, Theodore." Dr. Meyers looked into his

eyes. "By noon tomorrow, we'll have beds set up in the school gym for people with the flu. Unless your momma is dying, she's better off at home in bed, with you to take care of her."

Theodore couldn't believe what he was hearing. "But I don't know what to do for her!" His eyes began filling with tears. "What if she dies?"

"If her fever hasn't been high enough to make her mind wander, and she hasn't been coughing up blood, she'll likely make it to noon. Bring her to the gym if the fever hasn't broken by then."

"But I can't . . ."

Dr. Meyers put both hands on Theodore's shoulders. "You can and you will, young man. You can boil water to put steam into the air. You can give your mother lots to drink and you can keep her clean. A mustard plaster wouldn't hurt. Do you know how to make one?" Theodore nodded. "I'm telling you to do this because I know you can handle it." He squeezed Theodore's shoulders and gave him a push. "Now get out of here."

Dr. Meyers leaned down to help another flu victim and Theodore slowly walked out of the hospital. Outdoors, he looked up Station Street toward home.

No, he thought. I can't do it. I can't take care of them any more. Deep down inside, some part of him wanted to cry. Instead, he cut down an alley to the railroad tracks, and began running west. It was hard to see the wooden ties in the moonlight. He ran on between the silvery rails, watching his feet and counting the endless black ties, running away and away from the flu.

"Hey, boy!" At the shout, Theodore missed a step, and fell to the gravel beside the tracks. He rolled down a hill, over brambles and rocks. When he stopped, a strange man with red hair helped him up and brushed him off. "Where are you going in such a hurry?"

The man's strong hand held his arm and pushed him toward a campfire. By its flickering light, Theodore could see a circle of tramps. Some of the men were wrapped in torn blankets and some were under newspapers. One leaned against a dirty old cart. Theodore stared.

Irene had always told him that tramps were dirty and dangerous. She said they stole whatever they needed and killed if they had to. Theodore didn't know whether to believe her, but he did know that tramps were free. They could go anywhere they wanted to by jumping onto freight trains. Between trips they camped like this under the stars.

"I said, where you going, boy?" The tramp shook his arm.

"Montana," Theodore said, startling himself. He hadn't known where he'd been heading until he said it. West down these very tracks lay Montana. No more flu. No stink, no mess, and no fear. No one telling him to do things he wasn't ready for. "Montana," he repeated. "My aunt's got a ranch there."

"Come sit by the fire, boy." The redheaded man

settled down and patted the greasy blanket beside him. "I like you. I started riding the rails about your age, myself." He was studying Theodore in the dim light. "I'm Red," he finally said. "We're hopping a westbound freight at 5. You want to come?"

Theodore held his hands out to the warmth of the fire. In the flames, he saw the wide wheat fields and soaring gold mountains from the posters. *See the West by Train.* The words burned in his mind. This was his chance. In less than a week, he could be galloping across the ranch on horseback. He could tell that Red would get him there safely. He could almost feel the fresh wind against his face. "I'll go!" he cried.

"Momma!" a man's voice called from the bushes beyond the fire. Theodore's hair rose. "Momma, is that you?"

The men were quiet. Red spit onto the fire. "Don't pay him no mind. Bo's gone crazy." As the man in the bushes kept crying for his mother, Red said, "We're leaving him behind. He'll be dead before long, anyhow."

Theodore struggled to his feet and walked over to look. Bo wasn't any older than Everett. His face was shiny with sweat. His frightened eyes found Theodore's. "Help me," he pleaded. Theodore leaned down and felt Bo's forehead. It was far hotter than his mother's had ever been.

"Did you send for a doctor yet?" Theodore yelled back at the circle of tramps.

"I told you," Red said, "we're leaving." As a train-whistle blew, the tramps began gathering their blankets and gear.

Theodore stood, his eyes locked with Bo's. This could be Everett lying here, he thought. Or George. Or me.

"Come on, boy!" Red urged. The slow clackety rumble of the morning freight train filled the air. Theodore looked up the tracks toward the east, where a single headlight pierced the cold dawn sky.

"Don't bother with the new kid, Red," another tramp grumbled. "We don't need a baby still in his knickers."

The cuffs of Theodore's knickers felt suddenly tight at his knees. Blood rushed to his face in anger.

"Aren't any of you his friends?" he yelled at the tramps. The engine rolled past, hissing to a crawl to make a switch in the rails. "Stop!" Theodore's voice was hoarse. "You can't leave him to die!"

In the dim light, he could see the tramps leaping by twos and threes into open boxcar doors. Red was the last to hop on the train. As his car rattled slowly past, he leaned down and reached out a hand for Theodore. "You coming, friend?"

Instead of taking the hand, Theodore spat at the train, turned, and stalked back to Bo.

"I'll get you to a doctor," he promised as the freight cars rumbled out of sight. But first Theodore wanted to put out the tramps' fire. He spent a long time pounding every spark into darkness.

Bo was calling for his mother again. Theodore

begged him to try and help, but in the end, he had to pull and push Bo's sick body into the cart by himself. With a giant heave, he managed to roll the cart and its heavy burden over the rails and up into the alley.

He put his head down and leaned all his weight into the cart's handles to hurry it down the street toward the hospital. "What have you got there, son?" By dawn's light, Theodore saw first the shoes, then the pants, and then the jacket of a policeman.

"I've got to get Bo to a doctor," he panted without breaking stride.

"Why don't you let me take over?" The policeman jogged alongside.

Theodore shook his head no. He had to get Bo to the hospital. If he didn't, Bo might die.

"At least let me give you a hand," the policeman said.

Theodore shifted his grip so the policeman could grab one of the cart handles. "This your brother?" he asked as they fell into step.

"No, sir. I just found him by the tracks." Theodore didn't want to talk about Red and the other tramps now. Maybe never, he thought. With half of the cart's weight lifted, he could feel the soreness in his back. His legs felt wobbly and the cold air stung his throat. He tried to remember how long it had been since he'd had a night's sleep.

"Besides—" He didn't know whether he was arguing

with himself or the officer. "I can't stop until I know he's going to make it."

"Tell me where you live and I'll let you know what happens," the policeman promised.

At that, Theodore let go. He stood in the middle of the street watching the cart until it rounded a corner and vanished from sight.

With a deep sigh, Theodore turned toward the east. It was time to go home.

Long Pants

"Where *were* you, Teddy Bear?" Irene's angry voice woke Theodore from a sound sleep. "And *what* do you think you are doing in Papa's chair?" Theodore nearly swore until he looked at his sister, leaning against the bedroom door frame. Tear streaks stained her pale cheeks. Her hair was uncombed and her nightgown was dirty. She looked almost as sick as Bo had.

"What do you need?" he asked. She seemed startled by his lack of anger. So was he.

"Oh, Teddy, I feel awful. Momma's still asleep and I want her to be better. Somebody threw up on the floor and I'm too dizzy to clean it up." Theodore walked over to his sister and patted her arm awkwardly. "And Teddy, I'm so hungry." Tears filled her eyes as she leaned against him. Theodore wanted to pull away, but he remembered how Dr. Meyers acted with the sick people at the hospital.

"Let's get you back in bed." Theodore felt as if he were talking to a child. "I'll check on Momma and take care of the mess." Then he grinned at her. "And I'll trade you some milk toast for your Convalescent Cooking badge."

Instead of laughing, Irene began to cry. Theodore pulled the covers up as she climbed into bed, then felt his mother's forehead. It was cooler, and sweaty! "Irene!" he whispered. "Momma is better!"

But Irene didn't hear him. She was asleep.

Theodore stretched and wandered out to the kitchen. His clothes felt gritty, but more important, he was hungry. He lit a burner on the stove. There was no wild puff of flame this time. Mrs. Gordon should have seen that, he thought, pulling butter and milk from the icebox. He put the toast rack over the burner and heated slice after slice of Victory Bread, eating them as soon as they were warm.

The mail slot in the door rattled loudly in the quiet apartment. Theodore licked the butter off his fingers and went to see what the mailman had brought. He looked at the envelopes on the way back for more toast, but stopped when he read where the last one had come from. Montana!

As he felt the envelope, its dry glue cracked and the flap opened. Theodore knew he shouldn't read his mother's mail. But if it was good news, he argued with himself, he could read it to Momma when she woke up. He pulled out the letter. It might be just the thing to make Irene feel better, too. He sat down with another piece of toast and began to read.

"Dear Vivian," it began. The writing was sloppy. Theodore knew his aunt had been a schoolteacher before she married his uncle on the ranch. Her writing should be prettier. He read on.

"It is a sorrow to write this. The flu took Calvin yesterday." Theodore couldn't believe what he was reading. He looked at the date at the top of the page. It was a week and a half ago! "We sent him by train car to the hospital in Great Falls. He was wrapped in plenty of blankets, but fall is so cold here. They wouldn't let the sick folk ride inside a car, Vivian. They just put them on cots on a flatcar, and covered them all with a canvas to keep out the wind. I just weep . . ."

Theodore jammed the letter back into its envelope and threw it into a cupboard. He marched into his mother's bedroom, and wiped up the floor angrily. Next, he scrubbed the bathroom sink and toilet with a rag. The harder he worked, the less he could think about Calvin dying on the train. He swept the kitchen floor until he sneezed in the dust-filled air.

At last there was nothing left to do. He wandered

into his bedroom, trying not to look at the Montana posters. Theodore pulled off his filthy clothes and threw them into a heap. He stared at the clean knickers lying in his drawer. Never again, he thought. He put on a pair of long pants he found in Everett's dresser.

"Theodore," Irene's voice called from the bedroom. "Momma's awake."

Theodore hurried in to hug his mother. "You look great this morning," he lied. It seemed he couldn't tell the truth about anything. If he told her about Calvin, she might start coughing again, as she had when she heard about Everett. If he told her about Bo, she would be angry at him for being out all night. For leaving her alone. For talking to tramps. For having secrets.

Instead of talking, he went to work again. "Let's get you out of this bed, so I can change the sheets." He helped his sister get to their papa's chair and his mother to the sofa. Then he covered them both with blankets, and returned to attack the bedroom. First, he changed the sweat-soaked sheets. Then he wiped the tables and carried away the glasses and dirty towels that had been sitting for days.

"Theodore," his mother called. "There's a policeman here to see you." The astonishment in her voice was clear.

He wiped his hands dry as he walked to the living room. The officer told him that Bo was going to be fine. "But," he added, "Dr. Meyers said the boy would have died without your help." Irene gasped. Theodore

couldn't help grinning as he said good-bye to the policeman.

"Young man, I think you have some explaining to do," his mother said. The words were the same ones she'd used a thousand times before, but there was a new tone in her voice. Theodore liked the change.

"First I'll fix you both some milk toast," he said, and headed for the kitchen.

The next two weeks seemed like ages to Theodore, as he cleaned and cooked and cared for his patients. He bought them saltwater taffy with some of his Montana money and told them they were lazy as they lay about day after day. Neither woman could say the same about him. Theodore's work was dull, but every day his mother and Irene stayed awake a bit longer. They asked to hear again and again how he had saved Bo's life. He didn't mind. It kept them from asking if he had any other secrets.

One afternoon, Miss O'Reilley knocked at the door. Theodore didn't have much time to wonder why the ticket clerk had come. "I'm on my lunch break," she said, breathless. "I just got a call that your father is coming home on the 1:08 from Trenton." Theodore was pulling on his coat before she could say "Hurry!"

As they walked up Main Street toward the station, a man leaned out the drugstore door. "The war's over!" he yelled. "Praise God!" "It's over!" "It's over!" People began running out of shops. They leaned from the windows, screaming, "Hurray!" and "Thank God!" Church bells began to ring. Theodore and Miss O'Reilley pushed through the gathering crowd. Everyone seemed to be waving a flag, or a handkerchief, or a bottle.

A trolley full of cheering people rattled through the street and a train whistle blew down the tracks. "Hurry!" Miss O'Reilley said. The sidewalk was so crowded that they moved to the center of the street. It was worse there. Someone grabbed Miss O'Reilley and kissed her on the mouth. "It's over!" he yelled, thumping Theodore's back, and spilling beer on the road.

Theodore could see his father long before he could reach him through the crowd. He hadn't remembered his being so tall. They hugged and yelled "Hello!" at each other, but it was too noisy to hear anything. Motorcars were tooting their horns, "Aa-ooo-ga." Someone played "Over There" very badly on a bugle. Part of the crowd began singing "America" and Theodore realized many were crying.

Even though they couldn't talk in the roaring crowd, Theodore felt good with his father's arm around his shoulders. He remembered seeing Papa hug Everett that way. As they walked home, his father leaned on him more heavily. Theodore tried not to stumble as he realized how weak his father was. He looked up into the beloved face and saw lines of pain he hadn't remembered.

When they got to the apartment, his father stood straight again. Before they opened the door, he patted Theodore's head and said, "Thanks, Teddy!" Like a dog, Theodore thought, and pushed his hair flat again.

By the time he set his father's suitcases down in the bedroom, Irene and Momma were hugging Papa and crying. Theodore pushed past them to the kitchen. There would be time enough for him to talk later, he supposed. While he was making a pot of coffee, his father came in.

"You've been caring for them alone?" Theodore nodded. "Your mother says they were awfully sick."

"Most everybody was." Theodore moved to the other side of the table so his father couldn't ruffle his hair again. "Here," he said, taking the envelope from Montana out of the cupboard. "I didn't think Momma could handle this."

His father took the letter, glanced at it, then put it into his pocket. "We'll talk about it later," he said. "First we should celebrate. The war is over!"

During supper, Papa told stories of things he had seen in the war and in the hospital afterwards. Momma and Irene told him how Theodore had saved a life. Theodore wished they hadn't said anything. They made it sound like he was a hero. *Over There* was where real heroes were made. Theodore and his father put Momma and Irene to bed after supper. Papa sat in his chair and Theodore busied himself folding the blankets that were draped over the chairs and sofa.

"Theodore, I read the letter this afternoon and talked it over with your momma."

Theodore sat down hard. Now he knew he was in trouble. First, he had opened the letter. Then he had kept it secret.

"Did you read what it says?"

"Only the first part, Papa. I didn't think Momma was strong enough to know Calvin died."

"You were right not to tell her," said Papa.

I was? Theodore thought.

"But you didn't read the rest of the letter?" Papa asked.

Theodore shook his head. Maybe he'd be punished less for reading only part of a letter. He had told the truth, anyway.

"On the second page, your aunt invites you to come to Montana and work the ranch in Calvin's place."

Theodore stopped breathing.

"You've always wanted to go west. After all the work you've done here, we're willing." Papa cleared his throat. "Do you want to go?"

Theodore watched his father's tired face tighten as he tried to find a comfortable way to sit in his chair. Irene muttered in her sleep from the bedroom. A train whistle blew somewhere in the night.

"Can I go *next* fall instead?" he asked, finally.

"It's a promise." Papa smiled and shook Theodore's hand.

When you or I get the flu today, we are miserable for less than a week. There are medicines and hospital beds ready for us if we need them. The flu of 1918 was a different disease. It was not just miserable—it was deadly. There were no medicines to cure or treat it, and not enough hospital space. There weren't even enough coffins for the dead.

At least 22 million people died from the flu around the world. That is twice the number who died in all the fighting of World War I. Yet this flu epidemic isn't even mentioned in most history books!

The "influenza" showed up in many ways: high fevers, horrible coughing, vomiting, bloody noses, diarrhea, and quick deaths. Some people who caught the virus were dead within hours. The flu spread with frightening speed, too. One day a cook at Fort Riley, an army post in Kansas, complained of a fever and chills. By the end of the week, 522 of Fort Riley's soldiers were in the hospital.

Though the disease was called the "Spanish flu," nobody knows where it began. Soldiers traveling to battles spread the epidemic everywhere. People in their twenties and thirties seemed most likely to catch the flu, so many children had to care for sick parents.

My grandmother was the only member of her family who did not get sick. When her father died of the flu, she had to get a job to support her sick mother, brother, and sisters. She also had to do all the nursing and housekeeping for them. She was only 15.

She remembers how schools, churches, and factories closed to try to stop the flu from spreading from person to person. Parades and parties were outlawed. Dance halls and bars were closed, too, but nothing seemed to slow its spread.

What finally stopped the flu? No one knows, but the virus had infected people around the world before the epidemic was over. The worst had passed in America about the time World War I ended.

Like Theodore, my grandmother was walking down the street just as people heard about the end of the fighting. My other grandmother remembers weeks as a convalescent. Every afternoon her father read to her in his big leather chair. No one would come to visit them. There was no phone. No television. No one sent cards, for there was sickness in every home. It was a hard time.

Hard times can make heroes anywhere.

K.V.K.